PEDIATRIC
SUPERHEROES

BOOST & SUPER RUSTY

THE KINDNESS CRUSADERS

PEDIATRIC SUPERHEROES

ISBN: 978-0-6485-421-8-6
First Edition 2021

Published by GRABB Publishing
Design and illustrations provided by GRABB Publishing's creative team.

Dora Altintas
www.doraaltintas.com

DEDICATION

This book is dedicated to
the everyday and unsung heroes
that walk and live among us.

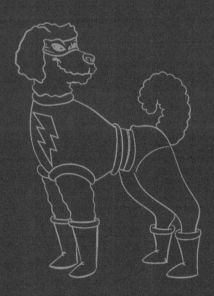

Standing atop a mountain as the sun began to set, Boost reflected on the day with his dog, Super Rusty.

"Another great day spreading kindness to others," Boost said with a smile.

Rusty barked and nuzzled Boost's hand with his nose. The bark told Boost he agreed, and the nuzzle meant he was hungry and looking for a treat.

Boost always kept his backpack handy for just such a request. He gave it a hard stare as it sat just a few feet away. The backpack's zipper, as if by magic, began to unzip. Then a treat floated out of the backpack, following Boost's strong gaze.

Telekinesis, the ability to move things with your mind, comes in quite handy when you're enjoying a sunset and don't want to get up to grab a dog treat.

"Here you go, Rusty. I want you to know that I'm proud of you and that you did a great job today," Boost said, as he flipped the treat into the air.

Boost and Rusty had an amazing relationship. They were like peanut butter and jelly, spaghetti and meatballs, fries and ketchup. They were just perfect together. Each was the only one that knew of the other's secret identity.

The warm rays of the sun began to fade. Boost knew his Mom would be calling him for dinner soon. The two best friends started off for home, making sure to switch back to their regular identities before they reached the front door.

"Back to Logan," said Boost, changing out of his incredibly cool superhero outfit. It looked like a leather jumpsuit you would wear to ride motorcross. It was green, bright blue and yellow.

The whole thing was topped off with a green helmet, complete with a mirrored visor. Rusty wore a matching green and blue outfit, with a green mask, and yellow lightning bolt on the chest.

During all their adventures they always focused on helping someone in need of a friend, a kind word or a bit of encouragement.

That was the one superpower that Logan and Rusty took with them into their regular lives. It's a superpower that we all possess and should use everyday, and that is kindness.

Everyone has their challenges to face. Some you can see and some you can't. But just because you can't see them doesn't mean they're not there and just as difficult as a physical challenge.

Logan knew all about having a challenge, because he has Cerebral Palsy.

Cerebral means that it involves the brain - Logan calls this a 'booboo' on his brain - and Palsy means a weakness or a problem with the way a person uses their muscles.

Cerebral Palsy affects people differently.

This is why Logan has braces on his legs to help him walk and has physical therapy to help him with muscle training, flexibility and balance.

But that would be the last thing you notice about Logan if you met him.

He is positive, caring, smart and so funny.

After a tasty dinner and a good night's sleep, it was time for another day of changing the world, one kind act at a time. Logan and Rusty ran into the backyard and once out of sight they became Boost and Super Rusty, Kindness Crusaders and all around super cool superheroes.

Boost launched himself high into the sky as Super Rusty ran below. They decided that morning that they would fly to the park and see if anyone there needed their help.

But that day they found out it's not only people that need a friend to look out for them.

Things around us need taking care of too. As Boost was soaring high above the park he spotted something that did not make him happy.

"This is totally unacceptable," said Boost. There was litter all over the playground area. Super Rusty barked and motioned to a nearby trash can. Boost used his telekinesis to pick up all the trash and put it in its proper place.

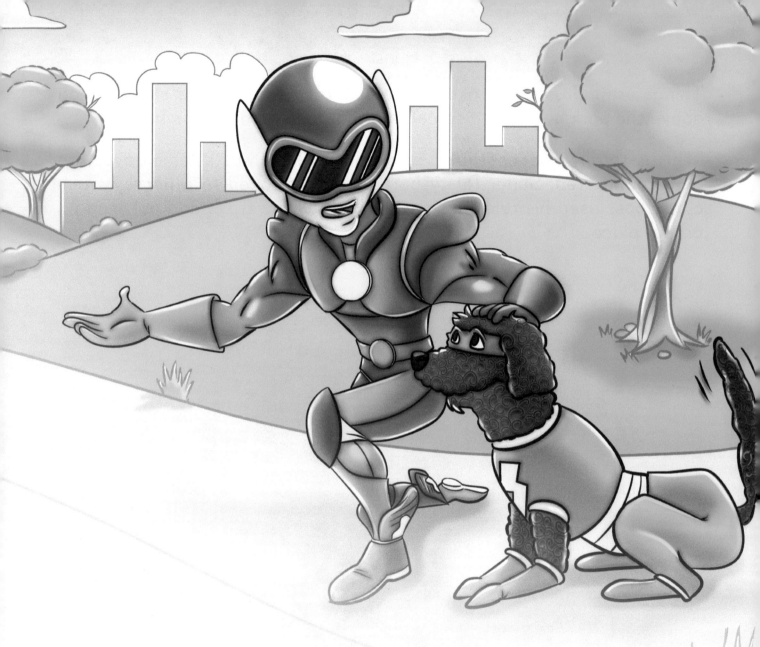

"We need to be kind to the Earth and animals too, Rusty," Boost said, as he finished up. "This park is home to so many animals. How would we like it if someone came and tossed trash in our house?"

Rusty thought a moment, and even though he did like nosing through the trash every once in a while, he would not want his house full of litter.

After they tidied up the playground, Super Rusty began to sniff the air and led Boost over to a little girl sitting alone on a bench. Super Rusty's special power was sensing when someone needed a friendly word or a little kindness.

Boost walked over to her and sat down. "Hi there, I'm Boost. How's your day going?"

"OK. But see those girls over there? I'm in their class at school. I'd love to play with them, but I'm just too shy to ask. Maybe I'll just head home," said the little girl with a sigh.

"What's your name?" Boost asked.

"It's Emily," she said.

Without another word Boost got up and walked over to the group of girls playing hopscotch.

"Hi, I'm Boost and I have a friend I'd like you to meet," he said motioning over to Emily.

"Oh, we know her," one of the girls said. "We go to school together."

Boost explained to them what Emily had told him, about being shy and feeling left out.

"Oh no, we thought she wanted to be alone," said one of the girls.

"But if you don't ask, you'll never know for sure," said Boost. "It's always better to ask and let the person answer for themselves. Rather than think you know what they want or what they're feeling.

Good communication and a kind word or action goes a long, long way."

He led the girls over to Emily and they asked if she wanted to join them for hopscotch. She was overjoyed and went to play, thanking Boost before she did.

"Great job, Super Rusty. Another win for the Kindness Crusaders!" Boost beamed.

They always felt so good showing others that, no matter who they are, they matter and make a big difference in the lives of the people around them.

The next day was Monday and Logan was off to school, with Rusty by his side. But as they rounded the corner Rusty started sniffing.

"What is it boy?" asked Logan. "Does someone need some kindness in their life?"

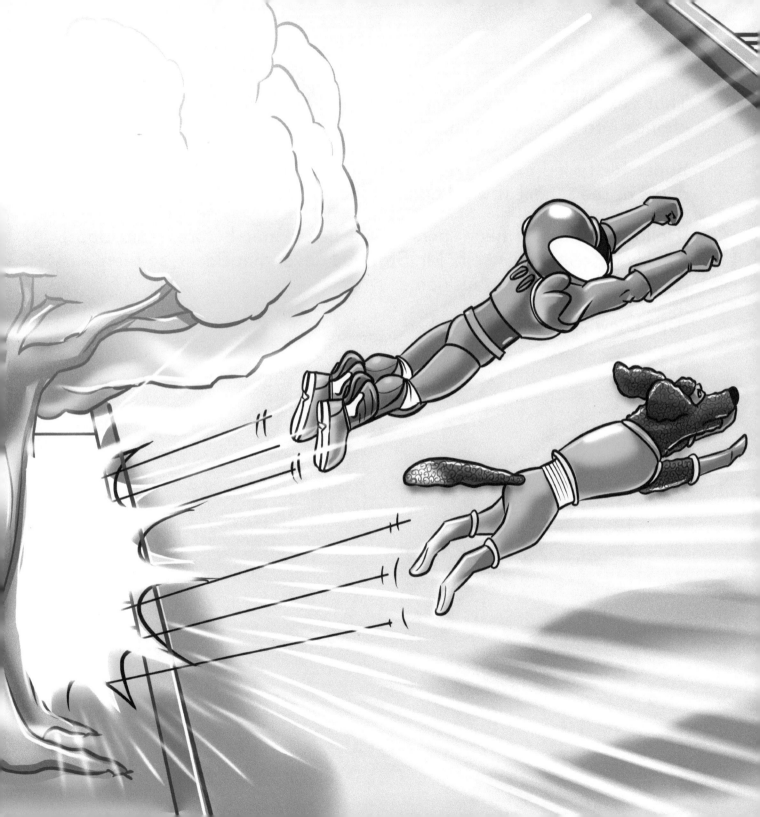

That's exactly what it was. The two superheroes darted behind a tree to change into Boost and Super Rusty.

Super Rusty led Boost over to a man standing just outside the front doors of the school. It was Logan's teacher, Mr. Star.

"Hello, Mr. Star....I mean, person I've never met before," said Boost, quickly correcting himself. Mr. Star had never met Boost, so there was no way for him to know his name.

"Do I know you?" Mr. Star asked.

Boost smiled and quickly changed the subject. "You look like you need a friend. Is everything OK?"

"Not really," started Mr. Star. "I left my back gate open and my dog ran off. He's done this before, but it's got me worried."

Boost looked down at Super Rusty, who knew exactly what to do. And off he ran to search for Mr. Star's dog.

"I know he'll be OK, Mr. Star," said Boost. "Maybe a joke will make you feel better. What do a house and a dog have in common?"

"What?" said Mr. Star with a smirk.

"A ROOF, ROOF," Boost barked.

"Good joke," laughed Mr. Star. "You remind me of this really funny boy in my class. His name is Logan."

"Logan? Nope, never heard of him," said Boost, as his face got red.

Then all of a sudden they heard some barking. It was getting louder and louder.

"Moon!" cried Mr. Star.

Moon was Mr. Star's dog. Super Rusty had found her!

"Thank you, Boost, for being so kind, making me laugh when I really needed it and having your amazing dog help find Moon. If you're not too busy, would you be able to talk with my class about the importance of kindness?" Mr. Star asked.

"I think I can," said Boost, not wanting to refuse the invitation.

"Great, see you inside," said Mr. Star carrying Moon, his new class mascot for the day.

"Oh, no!" Boost exclaimed. "How am I going to be Boost and Logan at the same time?"

He knew Mr. Star would notice if he wasn't in class. Then he came up with a plan.

He grabbed the hooded sweatshirt in his backpack, and looked at Super Rusty.

Mr. Star took attendance. "Logan," he called out. "Logan?" he said again.

Rusty let out a "Woof."

"Was that you, Moon?" asked Mr. Star. "No barking in class." He marked Logan present and moved on.

"Before we start class today," Mr. Star began. "I have a special guest to talk with you about the importance of being kind. Please say hello to Boost."

Boost then started to tell his class that they all can be every day superheroes. They don't need a cape or the ability to fly to make a difference.

"Kindness, respect and acceptance help to build a beautiful world," said Boost. "Those are my greatest super powers, and yours too."

At the end of his talk he, flew out of the classroom. Waving goodbye to his friends. Now he just needed to find a way back in....as Logan.

When Mr. Star turned his back to the class, Logan motioned to Rusty.

"Logan, where are you going?" whispered a friend. "And why are you going there on all fours?"

With Rusty out of the classroom, Logan switched into his t-shirt and snuck back in just as Mr. Star turned around.

"I hope everyone enjoyed that special message this morning and will try their hardest to be kind every day." said Mr. Star staring at Logan's desk.

"Logan, is that a motocross helmet in your backpack?" asked Mr. Star.

Logan quickly moved the backpack under his desk. "No, just my baseball helmet."

"Cool, it looks just like Boost's helmet, said Mr. Star as he started to teach their daily math lesson.

You too can be a superhero
and Kindness Crusader by remembering:

To be kind and respectful, because every body has challenge they may going through, and you may not always see it.

Smiles are infectious. See how many people you can pass your smile onto today.

Be helpful. Ask someone how you can help them today.

Show you care about your planet and environment by helping keep it clean and trash-free.

About Logan

Logan Foster was diagnosed with cerebral palsy at the age of two when his parents noticed delays with his right hand movements. He was unable to pick up items or make a closed fist and it was very difficult to dress him since he was born, always having to fish his arm through the sleeve.

Logan loves details. He is always dissecting everything he learns and wants to be an engineer.

He describes his cerebral palsy as a boo boo on his brain when showing his friends and family how he is different. Logan has worn braces on his feet since age two, in an effort to stabilize his feet and to prevent tripping. His right foot does not naturally swing back with each step.

When he was eight years old, Logan received Botox injections in his leg and hand to help lengthen his tendons. He attends occupational therapy and physical therapy for an hour each week. Logan is scheduled for surgery to complete a full reconstruction of his right foot which includes using two cadaver bones.

A sweet and witty kid who is always looking out for his peers, Logan was named "knight of the month" at his elementary school for showing acts of kindness. He will be the first to tell you that he does not like sports, but put a chess board in front of him and watch out because you will likely get beat.

Logan's motto is: "Everyone has something." This represents that everyone struggles. Whether it is a physical disability that you can see, an illness that isn't visible, or a mental health situation, everyone deals with challenges in life.

Life and Family with Logan

Being a parent is really hard; being a special needs parent is really hard and rewarding.

You have to instill the idea that being different is normal, while at the same time rallying behind your child to accept their differences and be brave enough to talk about them. It is when you see them comfortable in their own skin and accepting their differences that magic happens.

Our son Logan is a witty, snarky, kind young man. He is honest about his condition and openly talks about it to anyone that listens. He is brave enough to admit that he cannot do some things that other kids can, like riding a bike or getting both arms out of the water to do the freestyle stroke at swimming.

In our house, we teach our kids that everyone has something. Whether it is a physical disability or a struggle that is not visible to the eye, we need to realize that everyone is different, and that is ok. Empowering your kids to talk about their differences is so rewarding, because our differences are what makes us unique.

The most poignant example I can give is when Logan truly embraced his difference and unknown to us, he decided to take his cerebral palsy to school for show and tell. He bravely got up in front of the class, explained how he "has a booboo on his brain", and described his differences to his peers, showing them how the right side of his body reacts or does not react as it should.

His classmates were super engaged, and asked tons of questions to which Logan wittily replied in the way only he can, resulting in a lot of laughter. The bond he created that day with his class will forever live in our hearts, and the kids in that class.

Nicole Foster

What is Cerebral Palsy?

For kids with Cerebral Palsy, or CP, it can be harder to learn how to walk, talk, eat, or play. That's because people with CP have trouble controlling the muscles of the body. It could be a problem with the legs, the arms, or both. The word cerebral means it's a condition related to the brain. And palsy means a weakness or problem in the way someone moves.

Who can get CP?

No one knows for sure why Cerebral Palsy happens. In general, CP is caused by changes or injury to the brain around the time of birth through early childhood. For most kids with CP, the problem in the brain happens before birth, but doctors don't know the reason. It is not contagious, which means you can't catch it from anyone who has CP.

How is CP diagnosed?

Children with CP can have many different symptoms. Parts of their body may be very relaxed or very tight. This makes it harder to sit, crawl, or play. Doctors may order X-rays and other tests, and they will watch for changes as the child gets older. For a kid with CP, the problem with the brain will not get worse over time, and it will not spread to new body parts.

How can it be treated?

A kid with CP will have a team of doctors, therapists, and nurses who work together to find the best way to help. There are different types of therapy to help them develop skills like walking, swallowing, balance, and using their hands. Some people with CP have seizures, which are like lightning storms in the brain. Medicines and other treatments can help prevent seizures.

Some people with CP have twitching or jerking movements of their muscles. It's like when you get hiccups. Even when you try to stop it, the hiccups just happen. There are also medicines to help with this too. Sometimes, a special pump will deliver medicine to the spinal cord.

Children with CP may also be treated by doctors who specialize in bones and joints, the brain, the stomach and digestion, and other areas. There are a lot of people who want to help!

What is it like to live with CP?

Cerebral palsy usually doesn't keep kids from doing all the things kids do, like going to school, making friends, or having fun. But they might need special tools like leg braces or a wheelchair to help them move around. Or they may need some help with learning or daily tasks. If you want to help someone with CP, it's always best to ask first. The most important thing is to be a good friend.

Young Superheroes

We use superheroes to show young patients that the battles they are fighting make them strong and special. The first superhero ever created was a response to its creators being bullied – in this spirit, our superheroes fight issues young patients face during their time in the medical system.

Young people are meant to see themselves in our characters, to read one of our stories and recognize that what they're going through is also being experienced by the Young Superheroes ™.

Don't forget to get your copy of

BOOST & RUSTY'S: KINDNESS CRUSADERS

COLORING AND ACTIVITY BOOK

www.pediatricsuperheroes.com

Our Partners and Sponsors

It takes a superhero team to bring a vision to life, and the book you hold in your hand is a reality because of the support, ideas and power of our partners and sponsors.

*To our principal sponsor and partner of this project:
Dora Altintas and her creative team - thank you!*

Dora Altintas
www.doraaltintas.com

Bringing your book and vision to life by packaging expertise and stories into published books, products and programs.

The Published Authors Blueprint
GRABB Publishing

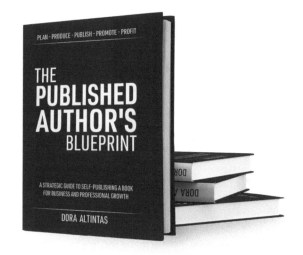

If you are interested in supporting or partnering with our upcoming Young Superheroes projects, contact us at: admin@pediatricsuperheroes.com

CPSIA information can be obtained
at www.ICGtesting.com
Printed in the USA
BVHW020803200921
617094BV00007B/300